P9-CKO-024

DRACULA

Text copyright © 2009 by Nicky Raven
Illustrations copyright © 2009 by Anne Yvonne Gilbert

All rights reserved. No part of this book may be reproduced, transmitted, or stored in an information retrieval system in any form or by any means, graphic, electronic, or mechanical, including photocopying, taping, and recording, without prior written permission from the publisher.

First U.S. edition 2010

Library of Congress Cataloging-in-Publication Data

Raven, Nicky.
Dracula / adapted by Nicky Raven ; illustrated by Anne Yvonne Gilbert. —1st U.S. ed.
p. cm.
Summary: A modern, illustrated retelling of the Bram Stoker classic, in which young Jonathan Harker first meets and then must destroy the vampire, Count Dracula, in order to save those closest to him.
ISBN 978-0-7636-4793-3
[1. Vampires—Fiction. 2. Transylvania (Romania)—Fiction. 3. Horror stories. 4. Stoker, Bram, 1847–1912. Dracula—Adaptations.] I. Gilbert, Anne Yvonne, ill. II. Stoker, Bram, 1847–1912. Dracula. III. Title. IV. Title: Dracula.

PZ7.R19552Br 2010
[Fic]—dc22 2009022116

10 11 12 13 14 15 16 GBL 10 9 8 7 6 5 4 3 2 1

Printed in Shenzhen, Guangdong, China

This book was typeset in Sabon.
The illustrations were done in pen and colored pencil.

Edited by Ruth Martin and Emma Goldhawk
Designed by Danny Nanos

TEMPLAR BOOKS

an imprint of
Candlewick Press
99 Dover Street
Somerville, Massachusetts 02144
www.candlewick.com

DRACULA

ADAPTED BY NICKY RAVEN

ILLUSTRATED BY ANNE YVONNE GILBERT

templar books
an imprint of Candlewick Press

Dear Reader,

I find myself in a quandary – that of turning Mr. Abraham Stoker's lengthy account of the sinister Count Dracula into a briefer story, some one-tenth the original length, for a younger audience.

How stimulating, but how challenging – indeed how presumptuous – to rewrite a literary classic in one's own style! But how to reduce such a detailed narrative by so much? Thoughts occur; Stoker's method of writing exclusively in diary entries and letters, whilst it offers great opportunity for a variety of viewpoints and authorial voices throughout the narrative, also leads to much repetition of events. Neither is his characterization altogether consistent; whilst the primary villain, the malevolent count, is a masterpiece of understated menace, many of the "good" characters, Holmwood and Lucy in particular, lack color. I shall have them married, and allow them a little happiness and passion. The Harkers, by contrast, I shall marry off later than Stoker does, to emphasize their loyalty and patience.

There is a mischievous spirit at work in many writers which leads them to revel in their most vile creations and imbue them with a charm and seductiveness lacking in the more virtuous. There was a real count in the Middle Ages who was a horror story all of his own. He was a prince in Wallachia (that's next to Transylvania, in modern-day Romania). He used to sit his victims on stakes dug into the ground, and their own body weight would push them downward, driving the stake up through their innards. How disgusting! They called him Vlad the Impaler, and he was no romantic Creature of the Night; he was a butcher.

If darkness of this blackest kind is to be vanquished, it must be met with wit and stout hearts. So, to Van Helsing I shall attribute much panache and a little levity – I cannot abide the sour-faced versions of Van Helsing offered to us by so many cinematic renditions of the tale. So too the gypsies; they were a persecuted people, and it is unthinkable they would ally with such as Dracula. I shall have my gypsies loyal and steadfast and an implacable foe to this Prince of Darkness.

I must leave you now, for my mind is racing and I must scribble again – create my Jonathan and my Quincey, my pale Lucy and my courageous Mina. I believe I shall dedicate this piece to my dear mother and her gypsy ancestors.

Your obedient servant,

NICKY RAVEN

Revenge (Prologue)

Like all his people in Transylvania, Pyotr had been brought up to hate and fear the Count of Castle Drakul. So, when the gypsy wise-woman told him that the time for their revenge was near, Pyotr felt a fire coursing through his blood. The tale of how Drakul had once hunted the gypsies for sport, and had come near to eradicating their line, had been passed down from generation to generation. Pyotr could hear in his head the stories told round the fires, of the desperate flight of the gypsy princess, Cristina, leader of the last rebellion against the count.

Cristina stumbled across the broken rocks on the hillside, the pain from the wound in her side making her sob at each jarring step. Not long now, she knew; the men with the dogs had picked up her scent at the foot of the hill and she could hear their clamour as they renewed their pursuit.

The rebellion had failed. All those carefully laid plans to overthrow this destroyer of souls, this monster impaler, this evil count, Dracula, had come to nothing. She tripped and cried out in agony, blacking out as the ground swelled up to meet her fall.

She came awake with a start when cold water was thrown on her face – she was not sure how long she had lain unconscious. She could feel a trickle of blood from a cut over her eye, and her ribs were throbbing. She was held fast between two strong men, and knew that it was pointless to struggle in her weakened state. As she lifted her head she found herself gazing into a pair of violet eyes. The eyes were narrow and cruel, set above a long aquiline nose in a gaunt face. Thin, unnervingly red lips parted in a hint of a smile. A smile that held no humour, only triumph and malice and danger.

The man spoke softly, an elegant and educated tone belying the viciousness of those eyes.

"You have been a worthy opponent, Cristina," said the count. His long, manicured fingers swept a straggle of hair from her face and he moved closer almost as if to kiss her. His hand brushed against the oval-shaped locket in the curve of her throat.

Cristina summoned a last shred of defiance and spat in the count's face.

"You can kill me, Vlad Dracula, but you can never kill an entire people," she hissed between teeth clenched in pain and fear.

The count smiled again in that expressionless way. "Kill you?" he said with a smile. "On the contrary, Cristina, I shall make you my queen."

Dracula leaned forward and, to her surprise, lapped with a sharp, pink tongue at the blood seeping from her forehead.

She shuddered inwardly at his touch, and braced herself for the humiliating assault she assumed would come next.

Dracula's mouth trailed down her face to her neck. Cristina couldn't stop herself glancing down; the count's mouth was open, and she noted in a strangely disinterested way his unnaturally long, needle-like canine teeth. She felt a searing pain as the count bit sharply into the soft flesh of her neck. She thought briefly of her young son on his way to exile and – she fervently hoped – safety, and then she passed out again. It would be the last warm thought she had.

Every day for the next three hundred years the gypsies waited for their moment to defeat the count at last; the moment when centuries of hate-filled dreams would be realised and peace would descend on the tribe once again.

June, a Business Trip

A carriage and team waited to conduct Jonathan on the last part of this long journey. Two lean, spare horses stood, stamping nervously, in the fog at the intersection where the carriage met the main stagecoach from town. Holding the reins of these fierce-looking animals was a man just as lean. He sat unmoving and erect, his cloak rippling around him as the chill breeze caught its tails. The driver's hood was pulled forward so it was difficult to see his face beyond a paleness of skin and sharpness of nose and jaw.

As Jonathan stepped off the stagecoach, one of his fellow passengers, an older woman with the look of a gypsy or some such travelling race pulled at his sleeve, and pressed a posy into his hand, muttering and nodding with a strange look in her eyes, a look that mixed fear and . . . what was it . . . ? Defiance? The driver's attendant had a fearful manner, too; he all but threw Jonathan's bags into the smaller carriage before scurrying back to his coach, crossing himself as he did so. The coachman picked up the reigns to his team of four, and called across to the silent newcomer in the guttural local dialect. The sharp-faced man's reply was barely a whisper, but the coachman must have heard it, for his brows furrowed and he spat on the ground before whipping his team down the trail.

Reflections

As the carriage rattled through the deepening gloom of the craggy and unwelcoming landscape, Jonathan reflected on the turn of events that had brought him to this strange place far away from his London lodgings. He twisted the old woman's posy around in his hands as his mind wandered, finding its herby, faintly minty smell strangely relaxing.

It was less than a month since the letter had arrived confirming that he, Jonathan Harker, was now a fully qualified solicitor-at-law. At much the same time, his mentor, Mr. Hawkins, had received the letter from Europe requesting that a London home be found for a prestigious and aristocratic client. Such a home – Carfax House – had been duly located and reserved for this client. A swift interchange of letters sealed the deal in principle and – Mr. Hawkins being a portly man and disinclined to travel – Jonathan had been dispatched to conclude the agreement.

Jonathan's excitement at being handed so important a task so early in his career was tempered by the fact that he would be away from his beloved Mina for the best part of six weeks. He smiled as he thought of Mina, her lightly angelic features and quick, clever mind. He grinned openly when he remembered her gasp of delight and instant consent when he had asked her to marry him.

Thoughts of marriage turned his mind to Mina's friend, Lucy, and her impending wedding. The husband-to-be was Arthur Holmwood, heir to an impressive estate near Whitby; an estate Arthur would inherit any day as his father was sick and dying. Though Mina would have loved Jonathan to be back in time for the wedding, Jonathan was secretly pleased to be away, for he never felt entirely comfortable amongst Holmwood and his wealthy friends.

ARRIVAL

Lost in his reverie, Jonathan was surprised to look up and see the walls of an imposing castle looming above the steep path they were climbing. It was an awesome gothic monstrosity, all turrets and towers and angles. As Jonathan gazed, one of the tall upper windows was thrown into stark relief by the light from a flaring oil lamp. Jonathan gasped as an apparition silhouetted itself in the light. He smiled inwardly and chastised his fanciful self as he realised it was merely a man standing looking outwards, arms stretched wide for support on the sides of the windows.

He had barely collected his thoughts before the wiry coachman dumped his bags unceremoniously in the hallway of the castle and stomped off to stable his horses. The hallway was grand and baronial, but cold and dusty. It reeked of disuse and vague scuttling sounds in the corner suggested smaller inhabitants had replaced many of the human ones. There were doors to each side and a wide, sweeping staircase ahead led to a balcony.

After a few minutes, as Jonathan was beginning to lose patience, the reverberating boom of a closing door echoed across the hall from the upper floor. He heard footsteps on the stone floor, and he looked upwards to the top of the imposing staircase.

If the staircase was imposing, the man about to descend it was doubly so. He was extravagantly tall, his height exaggerated by his position at the head of the stairs. The long black cloak, lined with purple silk, that cascaded from his shoulders, was the only thing that gave his figure any substance. Within the cloak all was leanness and angular bones, from the strangely sunken, almost concave chest down to the long, pale fingers and black-trousered legs. Above, a gaunt death-mask of a face stared fixedly down at Jonathan. Unblinking violet eyes held his, and the young man was simultaneously aware both of their clarity and beauty, and of the danger and power they betrayed.

"Welcome to my home," came a voice. "I am Count Dracula. Please follow me and I shall show you to your room."

To Jonathan's surprise, the voice came from right beside him – he had no memory of the count descending the stairs. Shaking his head and remembering his manners, Jonathan extended his hand and stammered his courtesies. "I am honoured, sir," he gasped, "my thanks for inviting me to your castle."

The hand that grasped his was papery dry and the bones felt brittle, but there was no mistaking the strength and purpose in the handshake.

"Tonight you will rest." There was no question in the count's voice, so Jonathan proffered no reply. "There is food and drink in your room."

After what seemed an interminable walk through the dusty stone corridors of the castle, Jonathan was shown into a surprisingly welcoming room, with a comfortable bed and pleasant furniture. The count bade him farewell with a curious admonition: "I would advise that you keep to your room after dark, Mr. Harker. Castle Drakul is not a comforting place at night."

How true the count's words would prove.

July, a Visit to the Newly-Weds

As Mina dozed on the long coach journey to Yorkshire, her mind flew back to Lucy's wedding a month before.

How beautiful her friend had looked! And how lavish the entertainment provided by her new husband. The food and drink had been plentiful and the company excellent; she had spent much of the day alongside Holmwood's friend Dr. Seward – or John, as he insisted she call him. He had proved a courteous escort, although strangely sad at times. He had caught her looking at him curiously during one of those pensive moments, and confided that he had once harboured hopes of marrying Lucy himself.

Wedding thoughts turned Mina's mind to Jonathan and her hopes for their future. She frowned involuntarily. She had not heard from her fiancé for near on a fortnight, after only two hastily scribbled missives from Transylvania. This was so unlike Jonathan that she had contacted his employer, only to find he too was away on business – no one knew where.

Mina's mood lightened immediately when she was met at the coaching station by Lucy. The brief journey back to Holmwood's house was a pleasant half hour of gossip and giggles. The Crescent House was a grand place, much grander even than the town house the Holmwoods kept in London. It took Mina a while to get over her initial discomfort with all the opulence and liveried servants, but she soon relaxed into the daily ritual of formal meals and walking and riding in the countryside. To her delight, The Crescent boasted a fine library and she eagerly devoured the contents of its shelves.

The days passed pleasantly, but each fresh one brought further anxiety as still no news of Jonathan came from his office in London. Mina was worried enough to wire her new friend, Dr. Seward, and beg him to visit Jonathan's office to check for news with Mr. Hawkins, Jonathan's employer.

Strange Happenings

The day after the wire was sent, a profoundly strange occurrence took place in Yorkshire. Mina and Lucy were walking in the gardens, grumbling about the turn in the weather and the heavy banks of cloud that hung over the house. Almost as if waiting for a cue, the heavens opened and rain lashed down, sending the ladies hurrying for the summer house. They watched with a mixture of fear and excitement as the most violent storm they had ever witnessed broke around them. Lightning crackled and spat and thunder boomed in their ears. The rain on the summer house was deafening and huge drops rolled down its glass panes like giants' tears.

Two footmen with a tarpaulin rescued them from their retreat; just as well, for the storm railed for another hour before finally blowing itself out over the sea. Holmwood's mother had excitedly told them about a shipwreck she'd seen, upon her return from Whitby. The townsfolk had watched from the quayside in horror as a boat foundered in the bay, listing to one side as lightning struck the rigging, then wallowing drunkenly before beginning its descent into the frothing water. The ship had seemed abandoned but many onlookers swore they saw a single, tall figure standing amidships, arms held aloft, seemingly immune to the power of the elements.

The next day brought even more dramatic news. The main body of the hull had come to rest barely a half-mile from the town. There was no sign of any survivors, and the lifeboats were still lashed to the deck. The cargo too, had proved bizarre: wooden caskets, forty-six of them, empty of goods but half-filled with earth.

And Strange News

The incident would keep the tongues of the townsfolk wagging for many weeks and months, but the next day Mina had news of her own which drove the shipwreck from her mind in an instant. She was sitting in the drawing room, reading, when a footman announced a visitor – for her!

"How exciting," smiled Lucy from her seat by the window.

Mina's puzzlement was answered when John Seward swept into the room. Lucy jumped up with a glad squeal and ran to embrace him; Mina settled for a more demure smile and handshake.

"I have news, Mina," announced Seward once he was settled in the chair opposite her own. "Although it is strange news indeed, and not at all what you would wish to hear."

Mina gasped and started to speak, but the doctor raised his hand. "No, Mina, not that, and my apologies for startling you. Of Jonathan himself I am afraid I have no news. It is his employer I am talking about."

"Mr. Hawkins?"

"The late Mr. Hawkins, I'm afraid," replied Seward gravely, and he recounted the strangest story.

"At your request, I visited Peter Hawkins' offices two days ago. Finding the office locked, I enquired at a neighbouring office, to be told the grim news that Hawkins had been found dead on the office floor some days previously. The police had removed the body with great secrecy and no one could shed any further light on this mysterious death. I have friends within the constabulary, so I pursued my inquiries with them, but met with dark muttering and a shaking of heads. The best I could discern was that Hawkins had died from numerous strange injuries to the head and upper body, but greater detail than that I was unable to obtain."

"Poor Mr. Hawkins," Mina sympathised. "He was a kind man, and very supportive of Jonathan."

"He deserved a better end," agreed Seward. Going on quickly before either of the ladies could speak, he said, "But that is not the end of the mystery. I managed to gain entry to the office, to see if there was any correspondence from Mr. Harker . . ."

At this Mina gave a little gasp of excitement and sat bolt upright – Seward knew then that he had encountered a girl of true worth and fierce loyalty. He smiled at Mina and continued his tale.

"I found only one brief, formal despatch to his employer. But what I also found was confirmation that his work abroad was finished. The client, one Count Dracula, has taken a London residence called Carfax, some few miles from the centre of town. There were shipping documents, too, for some caskets to be transported to the count's new residence."

"But nothing from Jonathan other than that?" asked Mina, a little desperately.

"I'm afraid not," replied Seward, frustrated that he could offer her no more comfort. "The documents indicate that the count's goods were dispatched to his London residence some time ago, so there must have been some unexpected hitch in Jonathan's return journey."

"This Count Dracula," asked Mina, "has anything been seen of him at his new residence? Could we not ask after Jonathan at this house of his?"

"Carfax? I thought of that, Miss Mina. The grounds of Carfax adjoin those of an asylum I often visit – the causes of instability and fracturing of the mind are an interest of mine. I used a visit to the asylum as an excuse to check if anyone was living at Carfax. There were signs of recent visitors, but no one was at home."

Sins of Omission

Seward omitted to add anything about a disturbing session with Renfield, a patient at the asylum. Renfield, a deeply troubled man, spoke of the imminent return of his 'master'. Renfield's wildness of eye and obvious fear led Seward to wonder whether this 'master' might be real, rather than just another of the creations of Renfield's broken psyche, as the doctors at the asylum believed. In the past Renfield's ravings had been incoherent and nonsensical – this tale had a curious logic and cogency, despite the man's obvious derangement of mind.

He omitted also to tell Mina how worried he truly was about Harker's non-appearance. Seward knew Harker by reputation as a solid and reliable sort, not the type to be so lax in communication.

And Another Little Secret

Lucy had been quiet throughout the doctor's story. She was thinking about an encounter she'd had on her walk the previous day.

Mina had been tired so Lucy had strolled alone along the bluff overlooking the cove where the ship had foundered recently. She had rounded a curve on the path and seen a tall man standing on the cliff's edge looking out to sea with a thoughtful expression. As she had passed – a little nervously, for strangers were unusual in this inaccessible spot – he'd turned and spoken to her.

"It is a wild and untameable thing, the sea," he had said, surprising Lucy. The stranger's face had looked equally wild and untameable, his long blond hair whipped by the wind and his stark cheekbones highlighting a pair of penetrating violet eyes.

"Why yes," she had stammered without thinking. "Yes, I suppose it can be very dangerous."

There was something about the stranger's eyes that had compelled Lucy to meet his gaze, for all that her instinct, not to say her breeding, bade her do otherwise. The hypnotic effect had evaporated as his face broke into a smile.

"Forgive my rudeness," he had said, in a visible, but fruitless, effort to look reassuring. "You must be Lady Holmwood. Allow me to introduce myself; I am Count Dracula, late of Transylvania, but soon to be resident in London."

"London?" Lucy had queried, unsure how to respond, and not thinking to question how he knew her identity already. "But this is . . ."

"A long way from London?" The count had completed her sentence for her. "I am here on a small business matter. A ship carrying a cargo of mine from my homeland was blown astray by a storm and foundered in this cove. I am here to arrange the collection of my goods. And to take in some of this fine sea air," he had finished, with a hollow laugh.

Lucy had been disturbed by the count, but in a curious way she felt herself fascinated by him. He had an aura about him, an undercurrent of persuasiveness, and she'd found him oddly attractive, despite his alien manner. "Oh I see," she had replied, feigning an ease she did not feel. "Well, whilst you are here, Count, you must come and visit." It had seemed odd to be inviting a complete stranger to her home, but at the same time she'd felt sure it was the right thing to do. "My husband has a house in London himself – maybe we could offer advice on your new life there."

"You are most kind," the count had given a bow as he spoke. "I would be delighted. Now if you will excuse me I have business in the town." With another bow he had strode away, his long legs carrying him into the distance in moments. Lucy felt faint after the encounter – almost as if she had drunk too much. Now, her head seemed full with thoughts that were only partly her own, and she still had her uneasy feeling – but the count had been charming and courteous, why should she be concerned? And he did have the most beautiful eyes, she admitted to herself, blushing despite the fact that she was alone.

Another Encounter

The next day it was Lucy who excused herself from the morning walk, claiming tiredness and keeping to her bed. Mina took her book and followed the usual path to the cliff-top. Just as her friend had done the previous day, she gave a nervous start as she rounded the curve on the path and saw a gaunt figure staring out to sea. The stranger turned as she neared, fixing upon her a penetrating stare from the most extraordinary violet eyes.

"Good morning, Miss," he greeted her without once taking his eyes from hers. Slightly afraid, but also somewhat affronted by this bold stranger with the foreign accent, Mina met his gaze firmly.

"Good morning, sir," she replied, hoping her voice betrayed none of the uncertainty she felt, facing this tall, imposing figure.

The man opened his mouth to speak, and then clearly thought better of it, for he closed it almost immediately. Instead he nodded to Mina and strode away down the far side of the path toward Whitby.

By the time Mina returned to the house, Arthur Holmwood was arrived from London, his business completed earlier than scheduled. Mina discovered him in the drawing room in deep conversation with John Seward. The two men didn't at first hear Mina enter and she caught a snatch of conversation before they spied her and forced levity into their tones.

"But John, she's so pale," said Holmwood, frowning.

"I agree, Arthur," replied Seward in the tone of his most reassuring bedside manner, "but many women assume that kind of pallor with any number of minor afflictions. Lucy herself is adamant that it is no more than a minor fatigue. Let her rest for a day and she will be well again, you'll see."

At this point Holmwood noticed Mina and rushed to greet her, his face wreathed in smiles that masked any concern he was feeling for Lucy. Tea was called for and they whiled away an hour or two talking of business and travel and the mysterious shipwreck in the bay.

Sleepless Nights

Upstairs, Lucy lay in bed, alternating between sleep and fitful daydreams. She was sweating profusely, but would not, in spite of the doctor's pleading, remove the heavy scarf from around her neck. For what would the doctor make of those two strange marks upon it? How would she explain the presence of what looked for all the world like two teeth-marks imprinted upon her flesh? Her fingers were drawn again and again to the marks, and each time she touched them she felt a prickling sensation on her skin, and heat coursed through her body. She felt as if a weight pressed down on her, and if she closed her eyes all she could see was intense violet with a black centre; the violet beckoned her and she reached for it . . . then all was red, her head swam and she fell again into comfortless sleep.

In her lucid moments she remembered finding it odd that she had woken that previous night to find her casement windows flung open. A vague and disquieting memory came to her, of a tapping at the window in the night, and a shadowy form, like a large bird or bat, flitting outside silhouetted through the curtains. She remembered dreaming standing on the bedroom floor in her nightdress with a mist billowing around her legs. Or was it not a dream, but a true memory – had she really awoken and opened the windows?

That night Holmwood ignored his friend's advice and stayed with his wife, cradling her head as she slept. Lucy moaned a little and stirred restlessly, but she slept the night and the following morning looked a little restored.

Mina had not had such a good night's sleep. Twice she had been awoken by some creature knocking at her window; the second time she had been disturbed she had pushed her feet into her slippers and taken a look through the glass. The moon had been large and pale, and she was stirred by its beauty. Mina had always been entranced by the moonlight, the way it shed light on the mysteries of the night. She had reached towards the window lock, needing to be closer, even to reach out and touch the moon. As she did so the spell was broken, as a huge shadow obliterated much of the light; it was nothing more than the shadow of a bat, its size exaggerated by the spectral light, but it made Mina shudder and she drew her shawl around her and returned to bed.

A Sickness in the Blood

The next day passed easily. Seward announced he would accompany Mina on her return to London the following day. Immediately after supper, Lucy said that she was fatigued and would take to her bed once again, and the others followed suit soon after; Holmwood to a spare room adjacent to Lucy's to give her complete rest. It took Mina a long while to find the peace to sleep, troubled as she was by her fiancé's disappearance and her friend's mystery illness. Having dropped off late into the night, she was still fast asleep when Seward pounded upon her door. Within an hour of being woken, however, her fatigue was put to one side and she was calmly playing nurse as Seward tended to a very pale and sick-looking Lucy.

Holmwood had woken Seward upon discovering Lucy lying atop her bedclothes, ghostly white and thrashing her limbs whilst emitting a soft, keening sound. Seward quickly surmised that though there was no evidence to show it, Lucy was suffering from a desperate shortage of blood. In the absence of a local hospital, Seward took it upon himself to perform a transfusion, and Holmwood immediately volunteered as a donor. Thus Mina, despite the protestations of both men that this was no theatre for a young lady, found herself passing Seward various implements from his bag and bandaging Holmwood's arm. The intervention was soon found to have been a wise one, as Lucy's colour immediately began to return, and her breathing became less frantic.

During the operation, when Lucy had still been feverish, Mina had moved to remove the scarf from around her friend's neck, thinking to ease her breathing. Seward caught her hand and frowned at her; she caught his eyes and asked a question with her own. The doctor glanced imperceptibly at Holmwood, who was grimacing as blood drained from his arm. Seeing him distracted, he drew back the scarf for the briefest moment. Beneath it were two puncture wounds that looked unmistakably like the marks that a pair of sharp canine teeth would make.

Send for Help

Later they sat around the table while Holmwood restored his energy with a large steak and a glass of wine, and Seward suggested their next move.

"Tonight, Arthur, it is imperative that you do not leave Lucy's side."

Holmwood assured Seward he would not, and continued, "Tomorrow my friend Quincey Morris – you will remember him from the wedding – the American gentleman with the extravagant whiskers?" Mina and the doctor nodded. "Well, he arrives for a long-planned visit, and he and I will take turns to watch over Lucy – Quincey is a sound man and will not let us down. He once asked Lucy for her hand himself – I swear he would lay down his life for her."

Seward patted Holmwood approvingly on the arm. "And you are sound, too, Arthur. I leave Lucy in good hands."

"But you will return soon?" asked Holmwood, looking beseechingly at the doctor. "You will come with help or a cure?"

"This is an affliction beyond my knowledge," Seward admitted, looking at Holmwood with sympathy. "There are things in play here that medical science does not prepare us for."

Holmwood put down his knife and fork and looked troubled.

"What do you mean, John?" he asked.

The doctor's tone was flat and matter of fact. "I am faced with a situation. Lucy has lost blood – a lot of blood, not a drop or two – and yet there is no evidence: no stain, no trail, no sign of violence, no sign of forced entry, no noise. If no obvious explanation offers itself, we must think differently."

"So what are our alternatives?" asked Holmwood, sounding increasingly alarmed at the direction the conversation was taking. "Some sort of voodoo or occult force at work?"

Seward merely raised an eyebrow.

"But you've always sneered at that notion, John, always claimed that there was nothing which could not be explained by science."

"Indeed I have," agreed Seward, "but when science fails, where are we to turn?"

Holmwood looked downcast – he had faith in his friend's knowledge and seemed lost now that Seward had admitted being confounded. The doctor saw the look and clapped Holmwood on the shoulder.

"Don't despair, Arthur, there are other avenues open to us. I know a man. I studied with him for a while in Amsterdam. He is a scientist, but he specialises in researching and explaining phenomena which are unknown to us. He is a good man, if somewhat unconventional – I'd like to wire him. This is exactly his sort of problem."

"Then do it. Do it today," urged Holmwood. "I will embrace anyone, however strange or unconventional, who can bring ease to my Lucy. What is his name, this occult doctor?"

"He is a professor, not a doctor," came the reply, "and his name is Abraham Van Helsing."

Transylvania – A Sacrifice

The gypsies had tried to warn the young foreigner when he arrived – but none of them knew the foreigner's tongue, and the flower posy old Magda had given him before he climbed into the count's carriage had meant nothing to him; how would a foreign city-dweller know that heather and mint and sage spell danger? Once the great barred gates clanged shut behind the carriage, what else could they do but wait and watch? So Pyotr watched and waited for his chance to put a spoke in the wheel of the count's designs.

At night he would often catch a glimpse of the young man in his room, silhouetted in the window, often pacing up and down in what seemed an agitated manner. Other nights the count would emerge, crawling up the walls from his window like a giant bug to sit on the parapet and survey his domain. Although he was well hidden, Pyotr could feel the intensity of those murderous violet eyes boring into him, urging him to show himself. The count knew the gypsies watched him – every night either his henchmen or the black dire-wolves he kept as pets patrolled the forest. Often a wolf would sniff the ground around the very tree in which Pyotr hid – he was glad they could not climb, just as he was glad the men could not smell so well. Pyotr learned to shut out the screams and howls and wails that emitted from that hellish building. He found it oddly satisfying that what had at first made his heart quail and spirits sink became reduced to mere background noise by familiarity.

The count left the castle nearly a month into Pyotr's vigil – but Pyotr soon had a message that the party which rattled through the gates in convoy one morning did not include the young foreigner, but four wagon-loads of coffins; the count aboard the first. So Pyotr's vigil continued – and his patience was rewarded some three nights after the count's departure.

The night was punctuated by the usual chorus of damnation from the castle, but this time with a slight difference, for more of the sounds were human, like a man shouting. As Pyotr listened intently, trying to distinguish one sound from another, an upper window was flung open and a wild figure appeared, framed by the light within. The window was just above the spot where Pyotr sat; the forest grew right to the base of the crag from which the castle wall rose – some of the branches of its massive trees reached out and touched the lower parts of the wall.

As Pyotr watched, the figure stepped into the window embrasure and turned to face the wall. Fumbling with his hands, the man felt, inch by inch, for a finger-hold. Pyotr held his breath as the figure left the safety of the ledge, driven on by whatever madness had seized him, and crawled with painful motion across the face of Castle Drakul. He was heading for the upper ledge of a lower window, and Pyotr saw the steam from his own breath as he exhaled with relief when the figure reached the temporary respite of the ledge.

Cursing himself for his forgetfulness, Pyotr swiftly climbed down from his perch in the treetops – the risk of detection was of small matter now. He cupped his hands and made three owlish hooting sounds into the forest, and then turned back, entranced by the man's slow progress down the castle wall. It was futile, he knew it, for there was only one more window embrasure on the way down, and then a sheer drop, with no visible handholds. And the man was no climber or acrobat – he had made it thus far out of sheer desperation.

The young man had just reached the sanctuary of the last window. Maybe it was the realisation that he had only completed the easy part of his escape, or maybe he allowed his body to relax, but he swayed once, reached in panic for the window frame, and then swayed outwards again, too far this time, and pitched from the wall. His backward motion took him away from the wall and towards the trees – Pyotr heard a grunt of pain as the body above him hit a branch. Looking up, he was showered with leaves and small branches and put his arms up reflexively to ward off the larger object that was approaching his head. The impact sent Pyotr crashing to the ground, but he was unhurt and quickly staggered to his feet. The body landed next to him, inert. He knelt beside it and listened; the man was unconscious, but he was alive.

It took an intricate network of contacts and sympathizers to escape the web of Count Dracula's influence and power. That very first night had been a close-run thing; had they not reached the river before the count's wolves they would have been tracked all night and surely found. Even after Dmitri's boat had taken them far downstream, it was a tense night – the count had spies and paid henchmen everywhere.

It had taken the gypsies many days to get the Englishman to the border and across into Hungary, from where their Magyar cousins had arranged for him to be taken to Budapest to recover from his ordeal. Word had finally come through that he was safe in a convent and slowly recovering his mind. Once they could find out exactly who he was, a message would be sent to the appropriate parties in England. The last part of the plan was to get word out that he, Pyotr, and he alone, was responsible for the abduction and had personally conducted the Englishman to the border – and only he knew where the man's escape route led.

The gypsies knew men would be sent to seize Pyotr and torture him and extract information, but they would never take him alive. Pyotr was ready and willing to die, for he had set the events in motion that would free his people and see the end of this accursed count at last. Eight of the count's men were sent to bring Pyotr in; only five returned to the castle with the body, one with a gunshot wound and another with a knife wound which would leave him dead by the morning. Pyotr died with a smile on his face.

September 3rd, Van Helsing Arrives

September 3rd proved a busy day. Mina awoke early and lay in bed, conscious that it was four months to the day since Jonathan had set off for Transylvania. She had returned to London three days before, and on the first of the month Dr. Seward had received a reply to his wire, dated the last day of August.

Your wire was expected. Agree – matter most urgent. We will join you in three days. Look to Miss Mina. AVH.

Seward had scarcely concealed his frustration at this delay. "Three days," he fumed, "it is no more than a day's journey from Amsterdam and I stressed the utmost urgency of our need. And who is the other party in this 'we' he talks about?"

Mina had shrugged by way of reply, having no answers, but soon another wire arrived.

Will arrive Waterloo Station on the 3rd. Quarter past noon. Bring Miss Mina and a carriage for four. AVH.

With these more precise instructions, Seward's mood improved and he set about making the arrangements, as well as sending notice to Holmwood that they would join him in Whitby within two days of Van Helsing's arrival.

By the time the doctor arrived with the carriage to collect Mina she was ready and waiting. Seward waved a piece of paper and as they travelled he read it to her. It was a wire from Holmwood; despite the best ministrations of Quincey, himself and his mother, who had volunteered to share nursing duties, Lucy's health was still in poor shape, and she declined daily.

Waterloo was a mass of carriages jostling for position amidst a sea of pedestrians entering and leaving the station. Seward and Mina gazed out across the crowds, although Mina, for her part, had no idea who she was looking for. They were so intent on their search that neither of them was aware of a door behind them opening, until a deep, crisp voice said in lightly accented English.

"We may join you, yes?"

Seward gasped and spun around, Mina too.

"Professor Van Helsing!" exclaimed the doctor. The face that beamed back at them was far from what Mina had expected. This was not the kind of professor she had read about or seen giving lectures – grey-haired mostly, kindly and academic, usually bearded. This man was lean and spare and muscular, with bony cheeks, a firm chin, and piercing blue eyes. He had no beard – indeed, he had no hair at all. The only thing which broke the lines of his face was a pair of spectacles perched on top of his not inconsiderable nose.

"The very same," smiled Van Helsing. "And may I introduce my companion – he has come all the way from Budapest to see you."

Van Helsing stepped aside and another face appeared in the doorway of the carriage. It was a face Mina knew well, if thinner and more harrowed. It was a face that had been in her thoughts and dreams every day for the last four months. It was the face she most wanted to see in the whole world. There, his pallid features wreathed in smiles, stood Jonathan Harker.

Mina wished she remembered more of the next hour, for she was sure she had never been happier in her whole life. Van Helsing and Doctor Seward talked of Lucy's plight and events at The Crescent, but Mina barely heard, she could only look in wonderment at Jonathan. That he was bone-weary was obvious and his eyes bore the trace of much suffering and horror, but he was alive.

ESCAPE FROM THE EAST

When Van Helsing began to tell of how he had found Jonathan, Mina mustered her concentration and listened intently.

"I have contacts across all of Europe; men who help with the fight, directly or indirectly. Word came to me that a young man was in Budapest, in a convent tended by the sisters. The one who brought word told me dark forces had followed him there, and that other agents of those forces were surely closing in on the young man."

"Dark forces?" asked Seward. "Isn't that a bit melodramatic, Professor?"

"Ah, my young friend. You have intelligence and skill and confidence, but you have not experience of the world. There are forces at work in this world, both for good and bad, that you and your science cannot begin to comprehend!"

"And you do?" quizzed Seward, raising an eyebrow.

"Comprehend them?" retorted the professor. "No. And I never will, for they are beyond man's understanding. But I know they are there, and I have learned to recognize their presence and many of their ways, so I am better able to defend myself against their influence."

"These forces," persisted Seward, "what . . . ?"

Van Helsing held up his hand. "In time, my dear John. You must let me finish my story, incredible as it may seem. Mr. Harker will vouch for all I tell you."

Seward glanced at Harker and received a tight nod by way of reply, as if it were a topic almost too painful for him to acknowledge. The doctor sat back and motioned Van Helsing to continue. Mina reached over, took Jonathan's hand and gave it a supportive squeeze, receiving a tired, but warm smile in response.

"I hastened to Budapest, for I had been hearing rumours that an ancient evil had stirred in the east of Europe. Many stories exist of a scourge in Transylvania which has plagued that unhappy land for centuries. I arrived in Budapest in time thankfully, and was able to steal Jonathan out from under the noses of those who sought him. The Sisters of St. Peta have a strong and deep faith, and it was that which held the dark at bay long enough for me to reach him. We owe them much."

"Is that all that protects us? Faith?" interjected Seward, doubt again entering his tone, for he was not a deeply religious man.

"Yes." Van Helsing's reply brooked no argument. "But faith takes many forms, John. My faith is in God, and I carry it in my heart and it sustains me. Yours is in your books and learning and allied to your courage it, too, is a strong staff. Jonathan's faith was in love," here he glanced at Mina and smiled. "And that is maybe the greatest protector of all."

Seward appeared to think for a moment, and then he nodded again and sat back once more to allow Van Helsing to speak. "The journey back was a battle. Our enemies harried us at every opportunity; we were lucky to escape in Vienna, and word came later that our hotel room in Prague was ransacked only hours after we left. Only once we had crossed into Germany and were amongst my friends and associates in Cologne did I finally feel safe. From there I hurried back to Amsterdam to check my library, leaving Jonathan to follow at a pace more suitable to his still frail condition – hence my delay in arriving. I felt it best to deliver Jonathan safely to Miss Mina before Doctor Seward and I continue onwards together."

REST AND RECUPERATION

Although it seemed an age, it was still the day of Jonathan's return when the indefatigable Van Helsing and John Seward caught the night train to Yorkshire. Mina was left to help Jonathan's recuperation, a task she accepted wholeheartedly and with relish. Van Helsing advised her that he needed three things in great abundance – hot sweet tea, sleep, and love.

Under her ministrations, Jonathan soon regained some colour and much of his strength. In those first few days he talked little, and said nothing of his ordeal. Whenever Mina tried to refer to his travels he would change the subject, or simply stare into the fire or at the ceiling. Mina was patient – Van Helsing had warned her not to press Jonathan for information, for his mind had been broken and full recovery was still in the balance.

A week after Seward and Van Helsing's departure, Jonathan and Mina received a letter from the doctor. Lucy's condition was not much changed; she had undergone two further blood transfusions, once with Quincey Morris as the donor, and once with Seward himself. Van Helsing had instituted a strict regime around the patient's bedchamber – garlic plants at the windows and strewn about the bed, the casements and shutters closed at night, and crucifixes hung on every wall.

Jonathan looked pale at this news. "It's him," he gasped and seized Mina by the shoulders. "He's coming, Mina, he means to take us all!" Jonathan lay back in his chair, shaking and sweating. Mina soothed his brow and sang gently to him. Moments later, he sat bolt upright, his face set in a determined expression.

"But he will not have you, Mina!" Jonathan shouted suddenly. "Not whilst I am alive."

Despite Mina's protests he heaved himself out of his chair and tottered to his bedroom, returning with a battered leather notebook.

"I don't care what Van Helsing says," said Jonathan, calmer now and resuming his place by the fire. "You must know what we are facing. You are strong and resourceful, and this is an enemy which we must each fight within our hearts, in our own way, man or woman." So saying he placed the book in her hands.

"My journal," he said, simply. "The telling of it is beyond me at present, but the reading of it is not beyond you, my love."

Harker's Journal

While Jonathan dozed, Mina settled in her chair and opened the journal he had given her. Her hands trembled slightly as she turned the pages. She knew she would find the contents disturbing, painful even, but equally she knew she must read them to understand both Jonathan's state of mind, and the nature of the evil they faced.

June 10th

After my arrival yesterday I was joined by the count at breakfast this morning. As at dinner last night, the count neither ate nor drank. Afterwards we retired to his study to discuss business; everything appeared straightforward, and the count was satisfied with all the arrangements Hawkins had made for him. I was excited at the prospect of completing my first assignment so easily, and so disappointed when the count informed me that he needed some time to look over the documents fully. It seems I am to be a guest in this strange place a little longer.

June 12th

I had a very disconcerting experience this morning. I was shaving in front of my hand mirror, as is my wont, thinking, as always, of my dearest Mina, when a voice came from behind me. It was the count, and he had entered my room without a sound. "This is not permitted," he hissed, and I spun round with a cry — the cry redoubled as my razor slipped and I suffered a cut to my jaw. As I stood, amazed, the count seized my hand-mirror, flung open the casement window and hurled the offending item onto the granite below. I was too shocked to respond, and backed away at the sight of the count's expression of intense, cold rage. I reached for a cloth to stem the flow of blood from the cut, but the count was quicker. His hand reached out and touched the spot where I bled with what felt almost like a caress. As he did so he ran a pink tongue across his bloodless lips and gave out a great sigh. With a transparent effort, he tore his hand away, and stalked from the room without another word.

I sat for a moment, shaking and wondering about the count's extraordinary behaviour. I wondered at his silent entry — why had I not seen him in the mirror? I had my back to the door, and the count's reflection should have been visible long before I heard his voice. And why had it never before occurred to me strange that the castle boasted no mirrors of any kind? I confess to being quite shaken by these considerations.

June 13th

Last night was my fourth night at the castle, and it started in much the same way as the previous three. I dined with the count, who retained the demeanour of a courteous host.

After supper I was escorted to my room, my head filled with fears and doubts. Sleep evaded me, as it had before, and the night-time cacophony of the castle — so quiet and still a place in the day — was, if anything, intensified. As I lay tossing in my bed I became aware of singing amidst the general melee of shrieks and groans and mad laughter. This was the first harmonious sound I had heard since I had arrived at the castle and it thrilled me. I strained to hear that beautiful voice, and without even realising it I found myself walking the corridors following the beatific sound to its origin.

I remember a door, a tall, arched double door, and I remember pushing the door open and peering in. There were the singers — not one, but three, singing in one voice, pure and ethereal. I remember falling into their embraces — such was their enthralling power that I went willingly, succumbing to their beauty and the thrill of those voices. One, a raven-haired beauty, caressed my face and soothed my brow. The others stroked my palms and pulled at my clothes. They spoke to me in comforting voices, occasionally giggling amongst themselves. I remember one asking, "Are you hungry, my sisters, shall we feed?"

Oblivious to the danger I was in, I remember a feeling of disappointment when a curt, harsh voice cut across the foggy bliss of soothing hands and gentle caresses.

"Stop!" demanded the count — for it was he. "How dare you intrude on my business? Leave!"

The dark girl hissed and bared her teeth, showing unnaturally long upper canines. The redhead mewled like a cat, and showed her fingernails — better say claws, for they were sharp and curved.

"You defy me?" roared the count. "Be gone!"

I recall a fleeting glimpse of a nightmare figure, eyes shining, cloak-wrapped arms spread wide like a giant bat, mouth open to show huge fangs — fangs that dripped a red viscous fluid. The rest is a blank; my next memory is of waking this morning on sheets thick with the rank smell of my own sweat. The door has been locked.

All these memories are hazy. Indeed, all is so calm again this morning that I am scarce able to credit the evidence of my own eyes. I pray that soon I may be away from this hellish place.

June 18th

Are my wits deserting me? Last night I swear that I looked from my window and saw the count emerge from h own rooms by the casement and crawl like a fly up the walls of his own castle. What kind of demon is this?

June 27th

Every morning I wake with a creeping fear upon me. I sleep fitfully, and the horrors of this place encroach on my dreams. My body feels soiled, as if unclean things have crawled across me in the night. My mind is never clear, as if a layer of gauze cloaks my brain, and my blood runs hot and cold, as if I am gripped by some nameless fever.

The days are quiet, but it seems I am a prisoner here. The count deigns not even to speak to me, and the outer doors are barred. My own room is locked behind me at night — and even if it were not, I would not dare roam these corridors after dark, paralysed as I am by fear of what lies outside my door. I have given the count letters to send home but I doubt they will ever reach their intended destination.

July 5th

The count has gone, and I am left here alone with only the denizens of the night for company. I cannot think clearly any longer, my mind is dulled with terror. My memories of England are weak and watery, and other bloody and carnal images flash vividly before my eyes. I fear I am lost and am about to engage in some desperate venture to be free of this inferno. Only the determination I find in my more lucid moments, to be reunited with my dear Mina, keeps my mind from breaking.

By the time Mina finished reading the journal, Jonathan was asleep in his chair. Mina sat for a while watching the rise and fall of his chest. She could not undo the damage that had been done to him, but she swore to herself that never again would she let him suffer so. It was like Van Helsing had said – her love would be as a shield.

VAMPIRES

Such was Van Helsing's energy and personality, that within twenty-four hours of his arrival, any casual observer at Holmwood's Yorkshire home would have assumed that he, and not Arthur Holmwood, was the master of the house. He had hustled and bustled through every room, inspecting each window and doorway, checking that his strict instructions for securing the home had been followed.

"Professor," asked Arthur nervously during a rare interlude. "Can you tell us exactly what we are protecting ourselves against?"

Van Helsing thought for a moment, and then nodded at Holmwood, pulling him into the drawing room. Summoning Seward and Quincey Morris, he sat them all down, and looked each one of them squarely in the eye.

"You are all brave young men, full of confidence and without fear," he stated. "I am older, I am also a brave man, I believe, but I am full of fear."

The others exchanged glances – already they had experience of these sombre little lectures Van Helsing liked to impart.

"Ah, you snigger," said Van Helsing with a smile, cutting short the ensuing chorus of protest with a raised hand. "And maybe you should. Maybe some of my fears are the fancies of a foolish old man. But this I know," and he leaned forward in conspiratorial fashion and spoke softly. "Not all the things your mothers dismissed as fairy stories are untrue. This scientific, progressive world of ours has not yet rid itself of monsters."

"Monsters?" this from Quincey.

"Yes, monsters," repeated Van Helsing. "Creatures that stalk in dark places and haunt us when we are sleeping. Do you believe in ghosts, gentlemen?"

The three younger men hesitated, and Seward was the first to speak. "I have heard testimonies from sources I believe I can trust," said the doctor, "but nothing in my experience teaches me that these things are possible."

"You think them the imaginative fancy of disordered minds?" Van Helsing stood and looked down at the three of them. "Gentlemen, put aside your skepticism. There are ghosts, there are werewolves, there are vampires. They are real, they are of our time, and they are here, close by, stalking us as we sleep."

Van Helsing's voice cut through the next storm of protest like the crack of a whip.

"Listen to me," he insisted. "How does a fit, healthy woman lose blood and become ill with no apparent sign of disease or infirmity? How does a locked room get opened in the dead of night if some force does not compel those within to unbar the locks themselves?"

He had the quiet he wanted and continued in a softer voice.

"Arthur," he looked at Holmwood with sadness in his eyes. "Your wife is sick and near to death. We must increase our vigilance and not allow her to fail. She is in thrall to a vampire, and twice she has succumbed to his thirst for blood. If she should succumb again she will die, and worse, far worse, she will return as one like him: a vampire, undead."

September 11th, A Wolf in the Night

Over the next few days they maintained a constant watch on Lucy. Her condition did not deteriorate that week, but nor did it improve. She was pale and weak as a kitten, and occasionally still shook with fever. The sleepless nights took their toll on the watchers who would jerk awake in the middle of the night in the armchair by Lucy's bed, cursing their weakness, and relieved to find no signs of disturbance.

Van Helsing pursued his investigations, sending wires to all parts in search of information. His only triumph was in tracking down the shipper responsible for the cargo washed up in Whitby bay. The mysterious caskets had, as they now suspected, been shipped to Carfax, the new London home of Count Dracula. Van Helsing's enquiries also uncovered a later, smaller shipment of three caskets, sent by train and carriage from Castle Drakul to Carfax, due to arrive in two days' time.

Eight days after his arrival, Van Helsing decided to take a flying visit to London with Seward. Using Seward's connection with the asylum next door, they would pay a visit to Carfax and endeavour to discover the contents of the last three caskets sent from the castle. It was a decision Van Helsing would bitterly regret.

The night Van Helsing left, an exhausted Arthur Holmwood took his place by his wife's bedside. An hour later he was woken by Lucy's mother, newly arrrived on a visit, and persuaded to take a proper rest, whilst she took his place by Lucy's bed. Had Holmwood – or Quincey – been less than dog-tired they would not have taken that risk. They slept deeply, and never heard Mrs. Westenra fussing in the next room, muttering to herself about "that silly man and his smelly plants" as she removed the

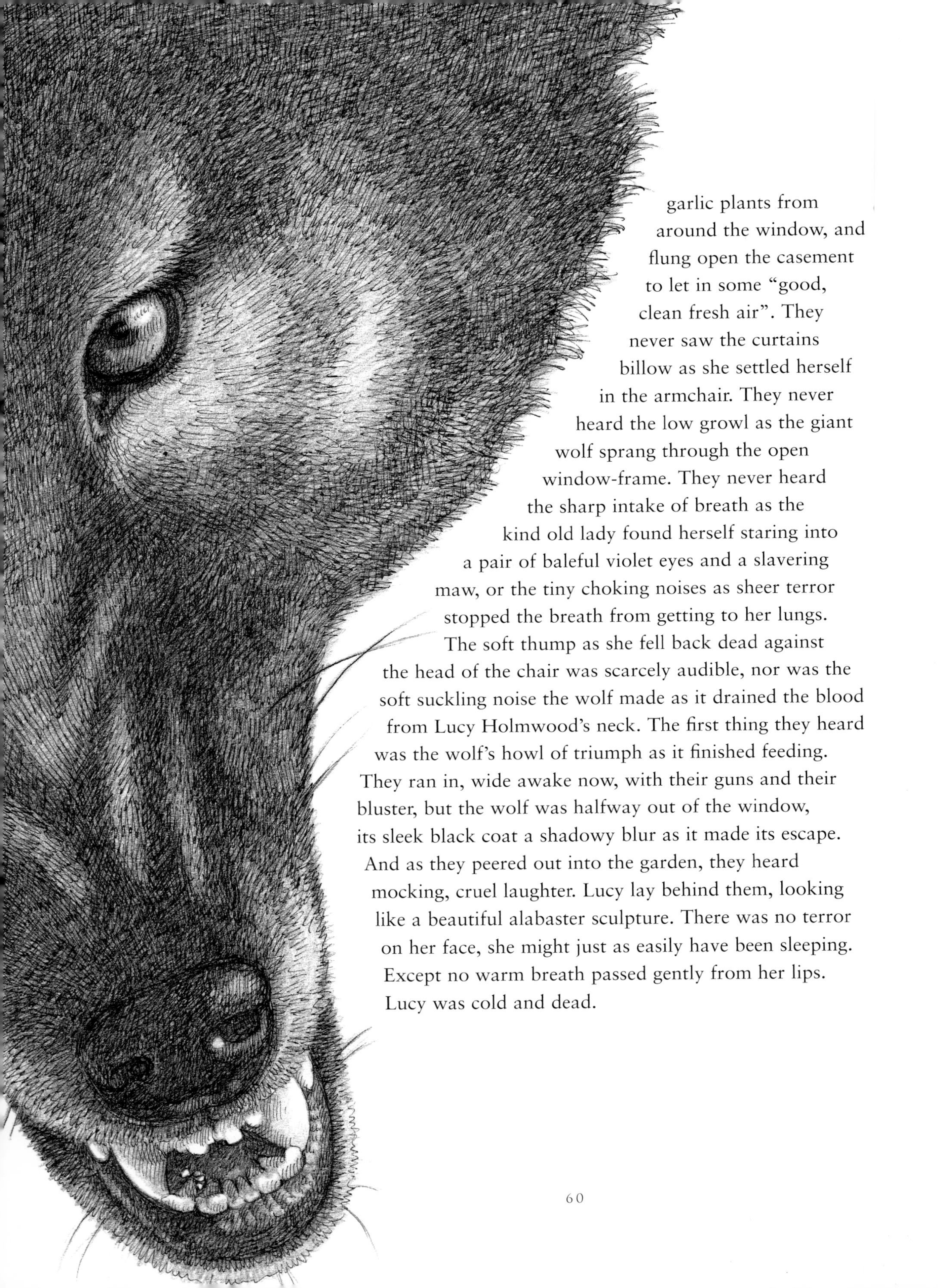

garlic plants from around the window, and flung open the casement to let in some "good, clean fresh air". They never saw the curtains billow as she settled herself in the armchair. They never heard the low growl as the giant wolf sprang through the open window-frame. They never heard the sharp intake of breath as the kind old lady found herself staring into a pair of baleful violet eyes and a slavering maw, or the tiny choking noises as sheer terror stopped the breath from getting to her lungs. The soft thump as she fell back dead against the head of the chair was scarcely audible, nor was the soft suckling noise the wolf made as it drained the blood from Lucy Holmwood's neck. The first thing they heard was the wolf's howl of triumph as it finished feeding. They ran in, wide awake now, with their guns and their bluster, but the wolf was halfway out of the window, its sleek black coat a shadowy blur as it made its escape. And as they peered out into the garden, they heard mocking, cruel laughter. Lucy lay behind them, looking like a beautiful alabaster sculpture. There was no terror on her face, she might just as easily have been sleeping. Except no warm breath passed gently from her lips. Lucy was cold and dead.

September 17th, The Seventh Day Approaches

Six days had passed since Lucy's death and three days since her funeral and interment in the Holmwood family crypt in London.

The six of them – Van Helsing, Seward, Holmwood, Quincey Morris, Jonathan, and Mina – were gathered at Holmwood's London house at Van Helsing's behest. In the wake of the tragedy, after the initial hysteria had abated, Van Helsing had asked for the support of the others in a mission to rid the world of this eater of souls, Count Dracula. There was not a hesitant voice among them.

Van Helsing looked around the table where they were taking supper, and nodded, seemingly satisfied with the calibre of his allies.

"This first part is in many ways the hardest," started Van Helsing, looking especially at Arthur. "Tomorrow night will be the seventh since dear Lucy's death. If she is tainted by this evil, as I suspect, then it is on the seventh night that her body will rise and she will join the undead."

Holmwood's mouth twitched; he was clearly struggling to maintain his composure. Quincey grasped his shoulder. "Courage, old man," whispered the American.

"The four of us will go to the crypt where Lucy's body lies at rest," continued Van Helsing.

"Four?" queried Jonathan.

"My friend," Van Helsing looked at him, "your spirit is strong but you are far from recovered from your ordeal at the castle." Jonathan looked Van Helsing squarely in the eye. "There will be five of us, Professor," he stated, quietly and effectively, "my part in this is not yet over."

Van Helsing paused and gave one of his characteristic nods of approval. "So be it. Five of us. Gentlemen, you must all bear arms – pistols, rifles, whatsoever you choose. Those of you who share my faith should wear a cross of some sort, or anoint yourself with holy water. Those men of science," this with a smile at John Seward, "must put up with the smell of the garlic!"

"What of Carfax, Professor?" asked Quincey. "Did you and John learn anything to our advantage when you were there?"

"Alas, no," replied Van Helsing. "We found Carfax empty. All I was able to achieve was to salt and sprinkle with Holy Water as many of the count's caskets as I could find. These casks are important – a vampire must have somewhere to retreat during the hours of daylight, so the casket is his sanctuary, and without it he cannot rest and gather his strength. Fifty were sent and we have destroyed many, so by our reckoning no more than six of the caskets remain unaccounted for. I have had the house watched and we know that a carriage – almost certainly containing the count – drove through the gates three days since. Any attempt on Carfax at this moment would be folly. The good doctor will tell you of what he saw next door in the asylum – but it is a tale for strong stomachs and whisky." This last was said with a twinkle in the eye and a nod to the decanter on the sideboard.

Duly fortified, they settled back at the table to hear the doctor's tale. Seward closed his eyes and related his ghastly encounter with Renfield earlier in the week.

Renfield Meets His Master

I arrived at the asylum at twilight and asked to see Renfield, an unhinged inmate whom I had been studying for some time. The last time I had seen him he had been raving about the arrival of his 'master' and the more I dwelled on this, the more it seemed to me that this master could only be the new owner of the great house next door – Count Dracula.

I was allowed into Renfield's cell, accompanied by a single officer – Renfield is potentially a dangerous man, and visitors are accompanied at all times. He sat in the corner, gibbering to himself and staring at something he held in his hands. As I drew close I saw this was a matchbox. I crouched in front of Renfield and he opened the matchbox, taking out a dead fly and dangling it between us.

"As flies to wanton boys are we to the gods," *he chanted.*

"Very good, Renfield," I replied. "King Lear is it not?"

Renfield looked angry at this. "There is only one true king!" he snapped, "and that is my master! He is the King of Shadow, the King of Beasts, the King of Blood. We are his followers and you will know us by the trail of dead!" All this was chanted, as if repeating a mantra, and it ended with a defiant nod of the head and the swallowing of the dead fly.

"Is your master close, Renfield?" I urged. "Is he here?"

Renfield's eyes bulged, and he looked over my right shoulder. I glanced around but there was nothing there.

"The master," this time it came as a whisper. Renfield started making odd gurgling noises in his throat and rocking backwards and forwards, his arms around his knees. After half a minute of this he moaned and looked up at the ceiling, "Forgive me, Master," he cried, repeating the phrase a number of times, each time more desperately than before, as if his plea for forgiveness went unheard.

I raised my voice to make myself heard over his cries. "Your master, Renfield, does he have a name?" And after a moment I added, "Is your master the Count Dracula?"

The instant I spoke the name, Renfield's rage mounted and he took on an apoplectic hue, snarling incoherently at me.

I instinctively backed away – and it was as well I did, for suddenly the madman had a knife in his hand. The knife swung, I put my arm up to defend myself and pushed myself backwards further, stumbling into the guard who had seen the sudden movement. My face was awash with blood, and it took a moment for me to realise it was not my own. I lowered my arm, which was soaked in hot red liquid and saw Renfield slumped back against the wall, his body still jerking, his throat torn open and blood still bubbling in an obscene fountain from the wound.

The doctor opened his eyes, and looked at his companions – none of them said a word for a few moments.

"Poor you," said Mina.

"And poor Renfield," added Jonathan, shuddering, knowing how close he had come to enslavement himself.

September 19th, A Stranger at the Door

Sleep came late to them all that night, so by the morning, the company around the breakfast table was taciturn and downcast. Each went about their business preparing themselves for the horrors that were to come. By mid afternoon, most of the men were out and about, with only Mina and Quincey Morris remaining at the house. There was a knock at the door, and a tall man cloaked against the autumn rain stood in the doorway.

"I have a package," he announced in clipped English, something similar to Van Helsing's.

"A package?" asked Mina, "I wasn't aware we were expecting anything."

"It is books for the professor," said the tall man, straggles of blond hair whipping across his face underneath his hat, "from Amsterdam."

How typical of Van Helsing, to want his personal library imported, thought Mina, and put out her hands.

"It is a heavy package, miss," said the delivery man, "where should I put it?"

Mina saw the box and it was indeed sizeable, so she ushered the man into the study, and bade him put it by the desk Van Helsing was using during his stay. The man dutifully obliged, backed out of the room and tipped his hat as he left.

Van Helsing was fuming when he returned from the city. "No wonder this city is prey to devils – hours it took me to find enough holy water for our purpose," he railed. "Do you have the timber, Mr. Harker?"

Jonathan nodded.

"And the garlic, Doctor Seward?"

"Enough to purge China," replied Seward with a grin. Van Helsing had stalked off to his room before Mina even had a chance to tell him about his books, and he remained locked within for the remainder of the evening, until it was time to leave for the crypt.

"Gentlemen," he barked, "we must depart. The guns are all loaded?"

Each checked their pistol, and Quincey the rifle he had stowed under his long coat.

"Then follow me!" and Van Helsing was out of the door, looking much like a fierce, bald general leading his troops into battle. Which, Mina reflected as she hugged Jonathan one last time, was something near the truth.

The cemetery where the Holmwood vault was to be found was to the North of the city, and by the time they reached it the clock had long since struck eleven. As they took up positions around the vault, Holmwood was clearly uncomfortable. Van Helsing and Quincey were the first into the vault, Quincey with rifle raised to his shoulder. The three behind heard Van Helsing curse and craned forward to see.

"As I feared, I dallied too long. We are late and already she walks abroad." They had never seen the professor so angry.

"What now?" It was Seward who asked the obvious question.

"We wait," came the answer. "Only the strongest undead can withstand the daylight; new-formed as she is Lucy must return here before dawn. Let us hope there are no innocent victims of my tardiness."

And so they waited. It was cold and damp in the cemetery and they were thankful for their coats and boots.

DREAMS

It was not nearly so cold at the house, but Mina slept only a little. She did not go to bed, but settled into an armchair by the fire and awaited the return of Jonathan and the others. As she slept she dreamed, but her dreams seemed the visions of someone drowning, not sleeping. Everything she saw seemed shrouded in mist.

She was walking the streets of London, uncloaked against the weather, and in her house slippers. She saw Lucy – surely it was Lucy – disappearing down a side street with a sweet-faced little girl holding a doll. As she watched them retreating into the mist, the doll fell to the floor and blood seeped from a wound in its neck.

In a doorway she saw Renfield's broken body lying in a pool of blood, hundreds of flies buzzing around him, flying in through his mouth and out again through the jagged wound in his throat.

She saw the professor opening a case like the one delivered earlier; he took off the lid and looked inside. There were books, old books, full of arcane secrets which would reveal all the hidden knowledge Van Helsing yearned to learn. As he lifted each book from the case it turned to ashes in his hands and fell at his feet.

Mina awoke with a start, panic in her breast. She felt weak, but at the same time strangely exhilarated. She remembered the books – why had she not made Van Helsing look at them? Who knows what help they may have been. She went to the study and opened the box – it was full of earth. On top of the earth lay a solitary rose, blackened and dead. Underneath the rose was a card. "For Mina," it read. She stood slowly, the weakness taking over, the singing in her blood receding. Walking to the mirror, she drew back her hair from her neck and stared, appalled but no longer surprised, at the two puncture marks in her clear skin.

AND NIGHTMARES

It was an hour before dawn when they caught a glimpse of white at the bottom end of the cemetery. Holmwood made as if to stir, but Van Helsing motioned them all to remain hidden. As the figure came closer they saw it was Lucy, dressed as on her wedding day, not as at her funeral. It was all Quincey could do to stop Holmwood crying out or running to her.

Van Helsing's eyes were on the small figure at Lucy's side, holding her hand. The child looked frightened but Lucy cajoled her onwards with soft words and promises. As she neared the vault Lucy picked up the child in her arms and carried her inside. At a signal from Van Helsing the five men surged to their feet and filled the doorway to the vault. The child stood, petrified with fear as Lucy bent over her, stroking her long fair hair back from her white neck.

"I cannot permit this," shouted Van Helsing.

Lucy turned to face the intruders with a hiss. Pistols were raised but Holmwood put himself between the guns and Lucy. "Wait," he cried – begged, rather. "Maybe she has rescued the girl, maybe . . ."

The creature that had once been Lucy Holmwood seized on this opportunity.

"Yes, that's right, my love," she purred. It was Lucy's voice but with a lascivious edge it had never had whilst she was alive. "Some horrid men were going to hurt this little girl, so I had to help her."

Holmwood stared at her as she approached him, more gliding over the hard stone of the crypt than walking; his face was a mixture of desperate, painful love for his wife and horror at what she had become.

"Get back," shouted Quincey Morris, raising his rifle. "Arthur, this is not Lucy!"

"Not Lucy?" crooned the monster. "Quincey, this from you! You who once professed to love me as much as my dear husband."

She moved towards Morris now, her hands reaching for her dress and starting to slip it seductively from her shoulders. “Here I am, Quincey, perhaps it should have been you I married, not my husband. You’re more of a man than he ever was . . .”

Quincey was transfixed – he, no more than Holmwood, could fire on the woman he had once loved. As her arms reached out to encircle him there was a cry of anguish and rage and grief from within the vault, and Lucy pitched forward violently into Quincey’s arms, the sharpened stake Holmwood had driven into her back jutting out through her breastbone. She sank to her knees, blood bubbling in her mouth, eyes looking beseechingly at her former husband. Van Helsing stepped forward, pushing the two younger men back, a long blade in his hand. He raised his arm and swept Lucy’s head from her shoulders with one long, clean swing. Holmwood fell to the ground, sobbing violently; Quincey turned away.

Seward and Harker helped the professor put the body of Lucy Holmwood back in its coffin, the stake still embedded in the heart. Van Helsing broke off the stake where it protruded, to make its removal almost impossible. The head was placed atop the body as decently as possible, and the mouth was stuffed with fresh garlic cloves and closed. Already, in true death, the long vampire canines had shrunk back.

The ritual complete, the party journeyed back to Holmwood’s house. The young girl was handed over to the authorities on the way; they hoped her innocence would protect her from the trauma of what she had seen. There was no elation, no sense of a job complete, just silence and reflection.

Brave Hearts

There was another shock to greet them when they returned. Mina was waiting in the hallway as they entered, her eyes red with weeping, but her face set in a determined expression. She drew back the scarf she was wearing and showed them the marks on her neck. Amidst the gasps of disbelief she stood, proud and erect, no shame in her bearing. Harker stepped forward and held the woman he loved as tightly as he could. The tears in his eyes betrayed the fierce pride he held in his heart for Mina's fearlessness and honesty.

"How?" asked Van Helsing behind him.

Mina pointed to the box beside the table in the hall, the box she had dragged all the way from the study.

Van Helsing went pale, and a stream of invective in no language the others knew issued forth. He beat his hands against his head and pounded the walls with his fists in frustration and impotent rage. It was Harker who spun him round and shook him by the shoulders.

"Professor," he spoke harshly, cutting through the older man's grief. "No one here is to blame. Evil, if left unchecked, will find a way to do further evil."

"Jonathan is right," this was Mina, adding her voice to his. "I will not sit by and be a plaything for this count, this Dracula. We must act."

Van Helsing had stopped ranting and was looking at his young accomplices in something close to admiration. For the first time that night he managed a smile.

"You are right, you young people," he told them. "All my schemes and plots and defences – where has it got us?" He took each of them by the hand and shook it warmly. "Thank you, my friends, for showing an old warrior the way. Yes, we must act. A new day has dawned, and tonight, we take the fight to Dracula."

"Tonight we end this," added Mina firmly.

"Tonight we end this," echoed the four young men together, their hearts and spirits lifted by a woman's courage.

September 20th, Carfax

It did not end that night.

Van Helsing planned well; he learned from his contact that Dracula, his business affairs in London completed, had booked space for three caskets aboard a ship from Dover the following day, and to make that boat he would be leaving Carfax shortly after ten o'clock in the evening. Further transport had been arranged for another three caskets a day later, so they would remain at Carfax until the following evening.

Van Helsing planned to have a carriage waiting outside Carfax from nine o'clock. They would wait concealed inside the carriage until the gates opened and then use the carriage to block the drive and afford undisturbed entry to the house.

It seemed Dracula had his intelligence, too, for at nine o'clock precisely, before Van Helsing's carriage had time to get in position, the gates of Carfax burst open and a landau emerged, the driver up on his feet urging the horses forward at full speed. Another, larger, carriage followed after, armed men aboard, and they had swept around a bend and out of sight before Van Helsing's carriage had even turned.

"Jonathan, Mina, with me," shouted Van Helsing, jumping down from the carriage and beating off the lackeys who had opened the gates. "You others, follow the count, but do NOT engage him. We will follow you to Dover as soon as we are done here – you must try and ascertain his route."

Seward nodded, and Quincey, who had the reins, whipped their team into a gallop and sped after the count's entourage.

Van Helsing looked around at his two young companions. "We three face a threat nearly as great as the count himself. Are you prepared?"

Mina and Jonathan looked at each other and smiled. They both looked back at Van Helsing and he beamed at them in a sudden burst of warmth. "By God, you two will have the most splendid children," he boomed. "Born warriors!" At this he strode off into Carfax chuckling to himself, with Mina and Jonathan hurrying behind.

Carfax was a grand mansion built around a central courtyard. Van Helsing strode through the main door into a hallway with a staircase leading off to the left. "We must go down," he asserted, "always down with these creatures, always the cellars."

They found what they sought in the kitchen area, a solid door with stone steps behind it leading down into the dark. Van Helsing took two small paraffin lamps from his bag, lit them and handed one each to Mina and Jonathan. He himself took a sconce that sat in a bracket by the door, and lit that from one of the lamps.

"There's something reassuringly weighty and medieval about these things," he mused. "This is good old-fashioned vampire hunting." He smiled at the young couple, who continued to wonder at his jocularity in the face of such peril.

"Professor?" Mina's voice made Van Helsing pause before descending the stairs. "What exactly are we looking for?"

"You have read Jonathan's journal?" came another question by way of reply.

"Yes."

"There are three caskets still here. You know what we face."

Mina went a little paler, then collected herself and pushed past the professor. "Then what are waiting for?" she demanded, starting down the stairs. The two men hurried after her, Van Helsing squeezing himself in front on the narrow descent.

The cellar was cold, and smelled of wine and damp wood and neglect. Amidst the empty wine barrels and racks of bottles were a few bits of old, broken furniture. Dominating the room was an enormous wooden table running its full length. In the gloom at the end of the table, beyond the light thrown by their lamps, was the vague outline of an arched doorway.

Ashes to Ashes

On the long table was an object which caught their attention. A wooden casket – to be more precise, a coffin – lay opened, with the lid cast negligently aside on the floor. Inside the casket lay what could easily have been a corpse; the beautiful, fair-haired corpse of a woman, in a wedding dress, maybe twenty-five years old, with a long aquiline nose and fine bones. The eyelids flickered, as if the body were about to awake, and Van Helsing moved quickly.

Seizing a stake from within his bag he ran forward and raised it in his right hand, transferring the sconce to his left. As the stake came down, the eyes of the blonde girl opened, and she screamed loudly and piercingly as she saw her last true death bearing down. Van Helsing stabbed downwards and without hesitation pulled out his blade and affected a scything slash; the screaming stopped. Mina moved to follow her instructions and stuff the mouth with garlic, just as she had heard Van Helsing had done with Lucy's body, but she stopped as she came close by the coffin and realized what was happening.

Just as Lucy's body had returned to its true state of a week-dead young woman, so this body returned to its true state. And this woman, by the style of her dress, was at least a hundred years old. Before Mina's eyes, the skin on the face tautened and pulled back, withering and falling away in a moment more. Within seconds she was gazing at the hollow eye sockets and bony hands of a skeleton, the dress hanging in rags around it. Seconds more and she was looking at a pile of dust.

"Ashes to ashes," whispered Mina.

"Dust to dust," echoed Jonathan.

A cry of "beware" from Van Helsing roused both from their morbid thoughts, and they held their lamps up towards the arched doorway.

Two figures stalked through the entrance – two more imposing, beautiful female figures, one with black hair and hard, almond-shaped eyes, the other with a prettier heart-shaped face and long auburn tresses. Their allure was unmistakable, their predatory hunger palpable.

The two advanced, floating like wraiths flexing long claw-like fingers and opening their lips to display their needle-like teeth.

"You disturbed our rest," said the red-haired vampire, in a petulant tone.

"Even worse," hissed the dark-haired figure, "you killed our sister."

"Worse for you that is," added the redhead, with a shiver of anticipated pleasure, "because now we're hungry."

Mina looked at Jonathan but not a flicker of emotion showed on his face. Van Helsing advanced, reaching for the crucifix around his neck, muttering Latin incantations. The black-haired vampire hissed and took half a pace back.

The redhead advanced towards Jonathan and Mina on the other side of the table, a malevolent smile playing across her lips. Harker put himself between Mina and the vampire and waited patiently for her to come closer, ignoring her taunts and seductive pouting.

Van Helsing tried to raise his crucifix, but it snagged against the collar of his greatcoat. The dark vampire snarled and knocked the cross out of his hands, at the same time catching the corner of his spectacles and knocking them to the floor. With a cry of triumph she ground the spectacles into the stone floor and looked up expectantly at the professor, who stood before her, stock still and seemingly lost without his glasses.

The red-haired vampire had used the opportunity to lunge at Jonathan, but he was ready; he stepped back quickly and the vampire was greeted with a wash of stinging holy water. She screamed in anguish and clutched at her face. From beneath his coat Jonathan produced a long, curved knife – Mina had never seen it before.

"A present from the gypsies," he said with a grim smile, and with a round-arm slash he severed that pretty head from its shoulders. Mina gasped in horror as the body, steaming from the holy water and drenched in blood, continued to advance towards Jonathan, and the head continued to hurl insults at them both, blood spewing from its mouth as it did. She knew what she must do, and closing her eyes, she put both hands around the stake she carried and plunged it into the sightless, still-moving torso.

Jonathan turned away immediately and looked to the professor. He still stood, transfixed, and the dark vampire caressed his face. "Poor old man," she crooned, "poor blind boy, is he lost without his glasses?"

At last, as the young couple watched in horror at what they thought was the end of their dear friend and mentor, Van Helsing spoke.

"I can't see," he said pitifully, "Is it dark in here?"

The dark vampire put back her head and shrieked with laughter, then looked back at Van Helsing, giggling maniacally. "I like this bit," she said, opening her mouth wide to bite, only to gag instead as a sticky, oily fluid covered her face and caught in her throat. Spluttering, she cleared her eyes and gaped in shock as Van Helsing, now far from immobile, grinned at her, his face lit sharply by the sconce he was carrying.

"I know," he replied, "let's have a little more light."

So saying, he touched the torch to the vampire's dress and she lit up like a bonfire, screaming in helpless rage until her vocal cords were burned away. The ghastly blackened shell of her mouth opened and closed once more, until that, too, was reduced to nothing more than ash, and she joined her sisters in a heap of dust on the floor.

Jonathan and Mina ran round to the professor, Harker pounding him on the back, and Mina seizing him in a most unladylike bear hug. As she did so, Mina spied something silver amongst the dust that had been the dark-haired vampire. She stopped to collect it and found an oval-shaped locket and chain; a locket containing a picture of the real woman whose soulless undead corpse they had just destroyed.

"Keep it," said Van Helsing softly. "It will remind you."

He looked earnestly at them both. "You did well, you two," he said, and then grinned broadly. "Born warriors!" he repeated with the same booming laugh as earlier. Then he stopped abruptly and resumed his earnest tone.

"We have no time to lose; we must follow the others to Dover as soon as we are able. Jonathan, you must find a carriage to take us out of London in ten minutes. In the meantime Miss Mina and I will consecrate this place and make sure it can never again be used for such foul purpose." With this he started off through the archway to the dimly lit back rooms. Jonathan hesitated, and Van Helsing shouted back over his shoulder. "Go, Mr. Harker, every minute is vital, and be assured I shall protect Miss Mina as if she were my own daughter."

Harker hugged Mina quickly and hurried up the stairs, leaving her to scurry after Van Helsing. "Professor?" she called after him, "what about your glasses?"

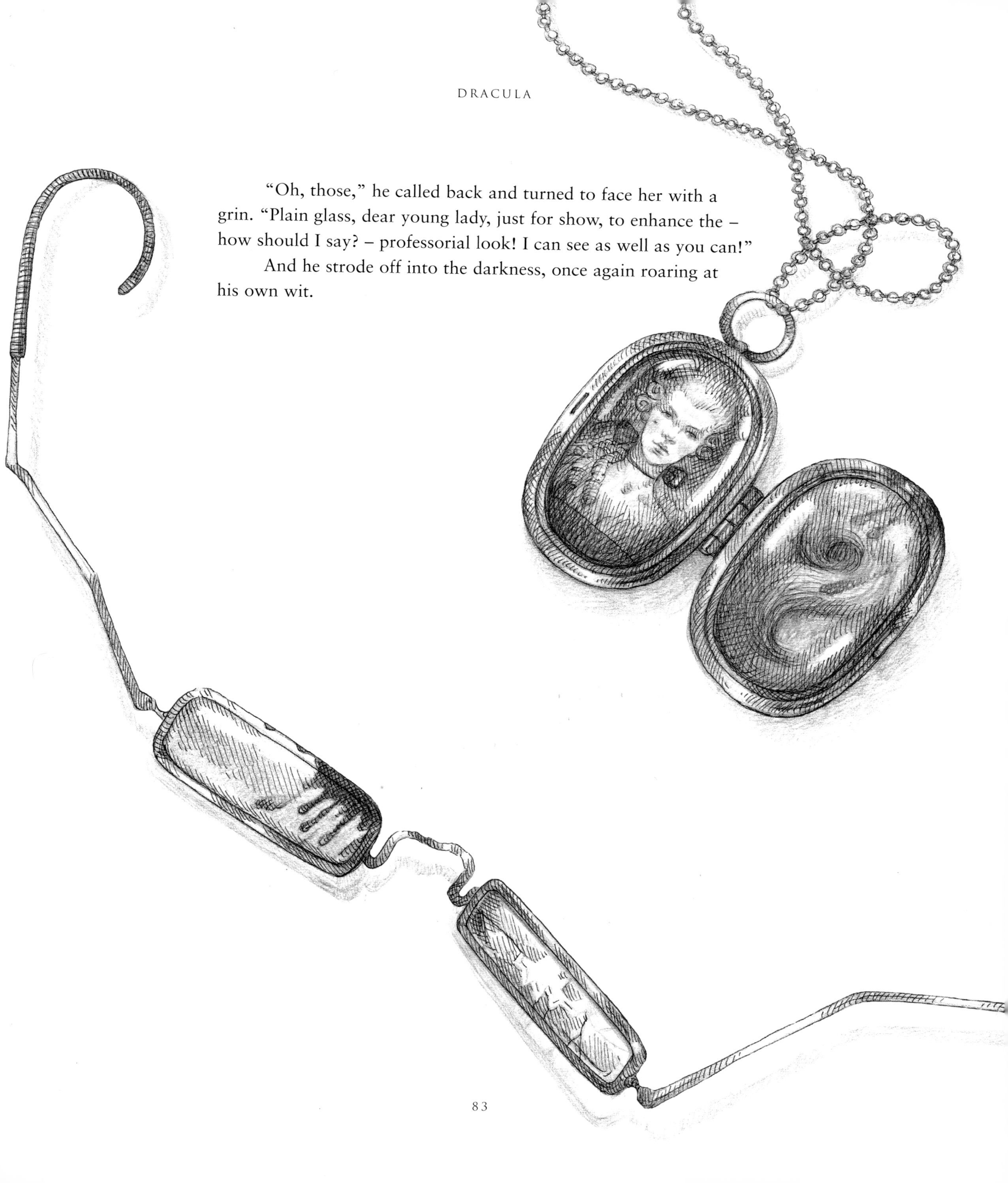

"Oh, those," he called back and turned to face her with a grin. "Plain glass, dear young lady, just for show, to enhance the – how should I say? – professorial look! I can see as well as you can!"

And he strode off into the darkness, once again roaring at his own wit.

Kill the King

It was the middle of the night before Van Helsing, Jonathan and Mina caught up with Seward, Holmwood, and Quincey Morris. They found them in bad temper, having just failed to head off the count at Dover. Their gloom was alleviated by the news of the destruction of Dracula's allies, but Van Helsing pointed out, in his pragmatic way, that Dracula could simply create more acolytes, so killing his conquests without destroying the count himself was ineffective.

"It is like the game of chess, my friends," he stated, "removing the opponent's pawns merely inconveniences him. To win the game, we must kill the king!"

Chasing Shadows

From John Seward's memoirs:

I believe Jonathan has kept a log of all our comings and goings in pursuit of the count after that night at Carfax, but I confess I find it all terribly confusing. We seemed to spend an eternity studying shipping logs and train timetables, and suffering interminable delays whilst Van Helsing arranged bribes and incentives for customs officers and shipping clerks.

We just missed the count at Dover on the night of the 20th – Arthur and Quincey were all for pursuing him on the next boat out, but I persuaded them to be restrained and stick to the professor's instructions. We did as he had asked and checked where the count's boat was bound, and were told the port of Varna – although none of us had the slightest idea where this was. Van Helsing, of course, did know, and assured us we could easily catch the count travelling by land to the same destination.

We made arrangements and set off on our way. During the continental train journey, after an uneventful crossing, a strange phenomenon turned the game in our favour. It seemed that Mina had an ability to sense the count's whereabouts, by which I mean not his specific location, but a sense of the atmosphere around him. By this means we were able to monitor whether he was on land, or at sea, or on horseback. Van Helsing believed that this asset had been gifted to us by the count himself – by biting Mina he had created an indelible link to his own person, and Mina's strong will allowed her to sense his presence without being overcome.

As we neared Varna, we learned this destination was a red herring and that the count would embark at another port – the name evades me at present. We would have lost the scent here had Mina not assured us that the count was most certainly still aboard a boat, by which the professor surmised that he was travelling up the Danube by barge. We could still cut him off if we travelled quickly overland from Budapest. We stopped briefly in that city to pay homage to the courage and healing skills of the Sisters of St. Peta, and then it was pell-mell across the hills of Southern Hungary into Transylvania. Once into the mountains we needed guides, and it was the gypsies to whom we turned.

As we travelled, our gypsy guide, who spoke something of the Germanic tongue in which Van Helsing was fluent, told us of the history between his people and Count Dracula. Dracula had once been Vlad Dracula, sometimes known as Vlad the Impaler, a tyrannical ruler of these lands in the fifteenth century. He had massacred many thousands of his people, and was especially savage in his treatment of the Romany peoples: the gypsies. He hunted them for sport, and almost succeeded in exterminating them entirely, until Cristina, the last gypsy princess, had rallied her people and organised a rebellion against the count. The rebellion failed, but Cristina's guidance had taught the gypsies the benefits of keeping to their old ways, moving constantly and never allowing themselves to be trapped in one place. And they have never forgotten her – even now, the gypsies watch Castle Drakul and aid any who encounter the dreaded vampire count, just as they aided Jonathan Harker. Most of us looked at Harker during the narrative, but he seemed detached now from the horrors that had beset him on his previous visit.

The atmosphere became very tense as we neared the crossroads where we intended to intercept the count's party. I looked around at my companions – we were a strange collection. Van Helsing, the man with a mission to rid the world of demons. Who was he really? None of us knew his history but we trusted him instinctively and he had not let us down. Arthur Holmwood; a man in torment who needed revenge and expiation for his wife's death. Quincey Morris; a good man in a crisis – I was glad he was with us. He, too, had loved Lucy and felt some responsibility for her death. Jonathan Harker; victim turned avenging angel, he looked nerveless and full of resolve. And Mina, brave, courageous Mina, destined to be Dracula's next bride if our desperate venture should fail. We must not fail! And I, John Seward, resolved to play my part, too; for months I had been an anchor for the turbulent ship of emotion this small group had become.

I was jerked out of my reverie by the cries of the others as we crested another rise on the stony path that wound through the mountains. A valley lay before us, and another path into the valley wound down from the opposite side of the ridge we were riding. Racing pell-mell down the other path were two teams of four, pulling carriages; both were decked with black cloth to hide the windows and both had riflemen mounted on the footplates and postillions.

We spurred our horses forward and raced for the junction of the two paths. As we rode I glanced down into the valley. The single path crossed the river at a bridge and then climbed steeply towards the forest on the other side. Above the line of the forest rose the towers of Castle Drakul, bleak and stark in the pale winter sun. On the other side of the bridge another carriage waited with fresh horses – if the count reached the bridge we were lost.

The first carriage turned down the single path moments before we reached it, but the second carriage stopped at the junction and the riflemen stepped off the foot-rails and took aim with their muskets. Van Helsing swerved off the path, cutting the corner across stony ground in pursuit of the first carriage.

"Doctor, Jonathan, Mina, with me!" roared Van Helsing.

Arthur and Quincey took their cue, and they and our gypsy guide pulled up their horses, and returned the first volley of fire from the riflemen. As I hauled my mount to the left, I caught sight of a body pitching forward off the carriage and rolling down the path – that Quincey was some marksman!

We were closing with the front carriage but it was almost at the bridge, where their reinforcements would bar our way. As we began to run out of hope and urged our horses to one last titanic effort, a marvellous thing happened. The spare carriage, which we had assumed was Dracula's, had drawn up, not facing the castle, but facing the bridge. The men on the cart threw off the black cloaks that the count's henchmen wore – and showed the woollen leggings and coloured neckties of our allies! More of them appeared from under the structure itself and from behind the scrubby bushes that bordered the river, and raised their rifles to their shoulders.

"Ai Pyotr!" they shouted, and unleashed a volley at the oncoming carriage. Forced to slow the carriage, the count's henchmen leapt down from their positions and rushed forward to do battle with the gypsies.

As we ourselves called our horses to a halt, the roof and sides of the carriage burst apart at the seams and there he was, huge and towering against the sun, hair whipping across his face, and his long arms clawing the air.

We halted. Dracula turned to face us and curled his lip when he saw Van Helsing.

"You ridiculous old man!" he snarled. "You think you know me? You know nothing. You are just food like the rest of this rabble."

"So bite me, Count!" taunted Van Helsing, advancing slowly with his cross held aloft. He was to the left, Mina and Jonathan in the centre, myself to the right, and trying to edge further that way to get myself out of the count's line of sight.

Dracula swung his gaze around the rest of us. "What are these you bring against me?" he spat contemptuously. "They are but children!" His gaze lingered on Mina and he licked his lips. "But this one, this pretty one, I will keep alive. So virtuous, so strong – they taste better when they are strong."

His violet eyes remained fixed on Mina, and she moved forward, her arms hanging lifelessly at her side. "Mina, no!" cried Jonathan, running forward to intercept her. The count moved with unbelievable speed, sending Jonathan spinning through the air with one violent blow and rounding on Van Helsing, who had charged him from the left, felling the old man with a slash of those cruelly taloned hands. Van Helsing fell, stunned and bleeding, while Dracula loomed above him.

He turned and beckoned Mina, and she came willingly, her eyes shining. "Now, old man, you will watch while I wed my latest bride."

I watched in horror, not yet close enough to strike, as Mina pulled the hair from her own neck, baring herself for a vampire's embrace. With a cry I hurled

my stake with all my strength. It struck the count in the back, but I knew instantly I had failed to find the heart. With a bellow of anger he turned to me, arms raised, and I saw my death in his eyes and closed my own.

When death failed to materialise I opened them again, and saw the count, still poised to strike, a look of disbelief on his face. Mina stood behind him, still holding the stake which she had driven through his body inches away from mine. As the count stood, frozen, Van Helsing staggered to his feet. Jonathan, too, had regained his feet, if stiffly, and was standing to my left in front of the still-petrified count.

"Never," said Van Helsing, gritting his teeth against the pain, "underestimate the children."

He nodded to Jonathan. Harker took the long gypsy knife from his coat and kissed it softly.

"Ai Pyotr," he whispered. And swung.

"Ashes to ashes," breathed Mina, moments later.

"Dust to dust," echoed Jonathan, and took her in his arms.

It Never Ends

There was a price to pay for the victory. The count's men had been unable to come upon them from behind, but Quincey Morris fell in valiant defence of the path. Even Van Helsing, hardened warrior, wept when he saw Quincey's body lying by the roadside. Holmwood was inconsolable; first his young wife and now his dearest friend taken from him. Quincey Morris had no immediate family, and so was buried in Transylvania, his coffin carried by Van Helsing, Harker, Holmwood and Seward past an honour guard of gypsy fighters – a tribute reserved for only the bravest and the best. He was put to rest next to Pyotr; two heroes side by side. The locket from Dracula's dark-haired bride, once the Princess Cristina, was buried with a new gypsy hero.

Jonathan and Mina were married, of course, and John Seward was best man at the wedding. Their children, Quincey and Lucy, became very fond of the doctor, and even fonder of "Grandpa Van" as the professor became known. Holmwood sold off the Whitby house, with its bad memories, and settled in London. He entered Parliament, and set up the Lucy Holmwood Trust for young orphans.

When Jonathan died in his fifties of a long-standing tubercular condition – a legacy of his horrors in Transylvania – Mina moved to the sea, to Cornwall. She would often be seen, walking the coastal path alone, looking out to sea, rubbing at a sore spot on her neck that never healed.

Seward outlived all the others. When old and grey he still visited his friend's children, now middle-aged themselves. He even passed away whilst visiting Quincey Harker, falling asleep in the summer house and never waking. His last memory was of Quincey's daughter, Cristina, bringing a young man to pay his respects to the old doctor.

"Uncle John," she said, "this is my fiancé, he is studying with me at the university. He is a law student."

"That's good," said Seward, "law is a good career. Does he have a name, your young man?"

The young man – a tall, handsome fellow with floppy blond hair stepped forward.

"I am honoured to meet you, sir," he said in ever so slightly accented English. "My name is Vladimir."

ANNE YVONNE GILBERT & DANNY NANOS

Anne Yvonne Gilbert – known as Yvonne – was born and raised in Northumberland, England. As a child, Yvonne was enthralled by the illustrations in the books of fairy tales that her mother would buy for her from yard sales. Little did she know the effect they would have. . . . Yvonne went on to study at the Newcastle College of Art and the Liverpool College of Art, becoming an illustrator in 1978. Her work has won many awards, and is held in the private collections of Arnold Schwarzenegger and the late HRH Princess Margaret.

Danny Nanos was born in Toronto, Canada, where he and Yvonne now live. Danny remembers being fascinated as a young boy by the dots on a printed page, especially when he realized that differently sized dots can create different tones of light and dark. He consequently became a graphic designer in 1985 and has since won many prestigious awards for his work.

Bram Stoker's *Dracula* is a book that means a great deal to Yvonne and Danny, who both see it chiefly as a love story rather than a work of horror. Yvonne relished the opportunity to make Count Dracula look very different, with his blond hair and purple eyes, while Danny brought light into a book that is normally dark in appearance by using white, uncluttered pages that allow the story and illustrations to spring to life.

This talented husband and wife team believe that "books are objects of beauty and art, to be treasured and cherished by their owners." Even now, Yvonne is still the proud owner of a copy of her favorite childhood book, a story about a cat named Nicholas Thomas, illustrated by Mary Kendal Lee.

Bram Stoker

Abraham Stoker was born in Ireland in 1847. He studied at Trinity College, Dublin, and then became a civil servant, writing stories and theatre reviews in his spare time. After marrying in 1878, Stoker moved to London, where he became business manager of the Lyceum Theatre and personal manager to the actor Henry Irving. He travelled the world while on tour with Irving, receiving two invitations to the White House.

Having spent several years researching vampire stories, Bram Stoker wrote his masterpiece and only work of any significance, *Dracula,* which was published in 1897. It went on to become one of the best-known horror novels of all time.